WHAM!
It's a Poetry Jam

WHJM!
It's a Poetry Jam

Discovering Performance Poetry

by Sara Holbrook

Foreword by Jane Yolen

WORDSONG

Honesdale, Pennsylvania

To Michael Salinger . . . just because
—SH

Like a true poetry jam, the making of this book was a team effort. My humble and heartfelt thanks to Jane Yolen for her vision and guidance, to Kent Brown for his nudging, and to Joan Hyman for her fine-tuning.

Wordsong
An Imprint of Boyds Mills Press, Inc.
815 Church Street
Honesdale, Pennsylvania 18431
Printed in China

The Library of Congress has cataloged the hardcover edition of this book as follows:

Library of Congress Cataloging-in-Publication Data

Holbrook, Sara.
Wham! it's a poetry jam : discovering performance poetry / by Sara
Holbrook ; foreword by Jane Yolen.—1st ed.
[56] p. : col. Ill. ; cm.
Summary: A guide to performing poetry alone and in groups; includes guidelines
to set up poetry-performance contests.
ISBN 1-56397-998-5
1. Children's poetry. 2. Performing arts in literature—Juvenile poetry.
(1. Poetry. 2. Performing arts in literature.) I. Holbrook, Sara.
II. Yolen, Jane. III. Title.
792.028 21 2001 CIP
2001094548
Paperback ISBN 978-1-59078-011-4

First edition
The text of this book is set in Minion.

10 9

CONTENTS

FOREWORD

I first met Sara Holbrook without knowing she was a poet. We were at a conference. She was a friend of a friend.

"Jane, Sara. Sara, Jane." Pudding, meet Alice.

And then I read her work.

Speaking of WHAM! Her poems hit me up one side of the head and down the other.

Then a year or so later, I heard her present her poems.

No, no, not *present*. That's too tame a word. Too weaselly, too simple, too small. She does not speak a poem or say a poem or even perform a poem. She sticks her hand down the poem's throat and pulls it inside out. She makes you laugh, cry, feel. She makes you want to hear that poem again, from the inside out and from the outside in. From the skinside, inside, from the inside outside.

We decided to work together. She sent me a gazillion poems (by actual count). I had the pleasure of helping her choose which ones to include in this book. Helping, not demanding. No one demands with Sara. You make a few suggestions and then . . .

Wham!

Get out of the way.

So, Pudding to Alice: Show them all how to go down the rabbit hole of poetry. I'll hold your coat. I'll watch your moves. I'll appreciate, advocate, congratulate, imitate, adulate. And after a while I will take a deep breath—and follow.

—JANE YOLEN

WHAM!

Loud
or quiet,
WHAM's a
screaming,
laughing,
clapping
word riot!

Don't tie poems to the page,
let them rage,
turn 'em loose.
Stomp, clomp, and growl,
then shake your caboose.

Be yourself, Paul Revere,
a crazy Mad Hatter,
a sad Mudville batter.
A rat or a ratter.
Add a far-out rhyme
to a flapping flamingo.
Zingo! Bingo!
It's sooner or lat-ter
a laughing matter.

Whether true or fictitious,
acting out poems
is both gross and delicious.

It's OK to keep score,
to whisper,
or roar.
Shaking words off the page
is never a bore!

Choose a poem of your own
or by somebody else.
Your major opponent
is always yourself.

Be a champ word-sport,
don't just sit on your hands.
Grab some poems
and some friends—

WHAM!
...it's a poetry jam.

Hey, you—poetry jammer!

Yes, I mean YOU!

Let me show you some poems that beg you to come out and play with them—some rappin'-tappin'-finger-snappin' rhymes for you to perform.

In a performance poetry jam, part of the fun is finding the power of your own voice.

Part of it is competition.

Part of it is acting seriously goofy. Part of it is never knowing what will happen next.

But I promise you one thing—a poetry jam is never boring!

Follow me from seat symphonies to solo performances, and soon you will want to perform poems you've written yourself. And so will your friends. And so will your class.

And that's when—WHAM!—you'll be ready to jam with poetry.

Make your poetry jump and jive.

Say it.

Move it.

Come alive.

Follow me. . . .

Do not commit your poems to pages alone.
Sing them, I pray you.

—Virgil*

---

*Who in the name of holey sweat socks is Virgil? He's a Roman poet who performed his poems to audiences more than two thousand years ago. And folks are still talking about him. That's some kind of poet performer.

Toot Your Own Horn

Tune up your voice instrument with the poem below. Notice it has a repeating line—also known as a refrain—and can be performed right from the safety of your desk. Hang onto your hats and eyeballs, the ride's about to begin.

Choose one, two, or eight jammers to read the verses of this poem, and have the entire class jam on the refrain. Don't hold back, now. Let's hear you loud and clear!

DOG DAZE

You think
the sun spots
are more bright?
The leashes
are less tight?
Over the fence
and down the street?

You think
there's not a single chore?
That nothing is a bore?
Over the fence
and down the street?

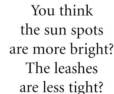

I'm tired
of my backyard,
I'm two paws up
and thinking hard.
Adventure
sure smells sweet.
Over the fence
and down the street.

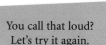

You call that loud?
Let's try it again.

11

Call and Response—a Class Act

When one person calls out a phrase and a group of people responds in unison, that is known as call and response. Poets and storytellers from Africa have used the call-and-response method of performance for so long that no one can even remember when it started. Way before there were newscasts and talk shows, before television, radio, or books, the poets and storytellers of Africa told the news of great hunts, wars, births, and deaths by performing poetry. And since these poets had no computers or even pens and paper, they memorized all their work.

The best thing about a call-and-response performance is that it gives everyone in the audience a chance to be part of the performance. And no one even has to leave his or her seat.

The poem "All My Fault?," on the next page, will help you learn two important skills for performance:

    1. the power of group response

    2. the power of memorizing

OK. I know what you're thinking: "MEMORIZE! Is she kidding?"

Here's the scoop about memorization: If you take the time to memorize a poem, you own it. You'll be able to express it better, and you'll give a better performance. Why? People can see your face, and you will be able to move more freely on stage.

Hey, it's not so hard. You know "Mary Had a Little Lamb," don't you?

How old were you when you memorized that?

You can do this.

Choose different jammers to perform the red "call" lines in this poem. Then have everybody join in on the blue "response" lines. This will be easy to memorize since everyone has only a line or two.

ALL MY FAULT?

The guinea pig has fleas,
there are grass stains on my knees,
AND IT'S ALL MY FAULT?
There's mustard on the floor,
and flies came in the door,
AND IT'S ALL MY FAULT?

The milk is warm and sour,
all the bread has been devoured.
THAT TOO IS ALL MY FAULT?
Why, when I walk into the room,
do you always start to fume
LIKE IT'S ALL MY FAULT?

Did I cause the national debt?
The creeping ozone threat?
IS *THAT* ALL MY FAULT?
How 'bout overpopulation?
Did I pollute the habitation?
IS *THAT* ALL MY FAULT?

Was I born to take the blame?
A guilty face to fit your frame?
LIKE, THIS IS ALL MY FAULT?
I didn't make the traffic slow,
but that delinquent video
is mine.
That one is all my fault.

Do you ever feel as if you are taking the rap for things that are not your fault?
How does that make you feel? You want to shout about it, right? Put the record straight.
But what if something *is* your fault. How many decibels do you want to put behind
your confession?
Use your voice volume control to communicate emotion in your performance.

Playing Catch with Words

Better close the classroom door for this exercise. And make sure your shoelaces are tied!

Partner up with another jammer. Stand face-to-face and repeat the poem "To Be" below.

Now, each of you take a giant step backward. Repeat the poem again. Notice how you have to project your voice a little louder to be heard.

OK, take another giant step backward—both of you. Say the poem again. Louder now. Keep backing up until you are a full room apart. Coach each other on volume control. Now you know how loud you have to toot your horn to be heard at the back of the room.

TO BE

I am
you see.
I am
what's me.
I am
not done.
I am
to be.

Another exercise is to turn this poem into a round. It's best to have a conductor for this. Divide the classroom into three sections. Have the conductor direct the jammers in section one to start, then the jammers in sections two and three should join in. This will give you experience in keeping your place while performing when other jammers are tooting their own horns.

Part of a good performance is being loud enough. But always remember, there is a lot of power in talking softly, too. Sometimes an audience will listen even more closely when the performer talks in a quiet voice. But it's disaster when you speak so softly that no one can hear you. A good performance will vary in tone and volume.

You've Got Rhythm

Ever heard something like this?

	one	a	ing		and	comes	like
Some-	reads	rhym-	poem	it		out	this. . . .

When you recite a rhyming poem, you shouldn't sound as if you are bouncing on a bucking bronco. You want to ride the words as smoothly as you can. This takes some practice.

Partner up with another poetry jammer, and talk the first verse of "The Dog Ate My Homework"(page 16) to each other. Read it as you would a story, not a poem.

Jammer One:	"The dog ate my homework."
Jammer Two:	"You've heard that before?"
Jammer One:	"This one ate the table,"
Jammer Two:	"then chewed through the door."

Not bad. Now switch parts, and try it again. No bouncing!

Now try tooting your horns in unison while bending the poem to fit a different rhythm. Can you sing this poem to the tune of "On Top of Old Smoky"?

Wow! It's a seat symphony.

THE DOG ATE MY HOMEWORK

The dog ate my homework.
You've heard that before?
This one ate the table,
then chewed through the door.

Broke into the living room
with his munch mouth,
snacked on some carpet,
and lunched on the couch.

He chewed up some albums,
then swallowed the mail,
even ate pretzels,
though they were stale.

He garbaged down everything
left in his path
and still wasn't full
when he found my math.

He chewed tops off bottles,
then drank all the pop.
As far as I know,
he still hasn't stopped.

If you don't believe me,
then give Mom a call,
if she still has a kitchen
or phone on the wall.

She'll answer and tell you
my story is true.
The dog ate my homework.
What could I do?

You can improvise with this one. Add or subtract a few beats, or see if you can
find another tune that fits the poem. Maybe you can even make a rap out of it.

Up and at 'Em

This is a lesson in movement. That means you are going to move. (No slouching. That means you!) Choose one or two jammers to read "Wham-a-bama One-Man Band" aloud, pausing after each activity so that everyone else in the group can act out the poem. Like this:

"I can stomp like marching boots." (**Everybody stomps.**)
"I can *ringle-jingle toot-a-hoot*." (**Everybody toots their air horns.**)

A poetry performance consists of words and movement. As a performer, you need to feel comfortable moving your arms, feet, and body. This should help you get started.

WHAM-A-BAMA ONE-MAN BAND

I can stomp
like marching boots.
I can *ringle-jingle*
toot-a-hoot.
I can *dum-ta-trum-dum*
anything.
I can clatter, chatter
chink-a-ching.
I can *clap-a-tap-a*
railing sticks,
play my tummy,
play my lips.

I can cymbal-bimble
lids-a-pans,
howl like sirens,
clap my hands.

I can buzz.
I can bam.
I can whistle.
I can slam.
If you listen
once to me,
there's no doubt
you will agree.

That none's
a louder sounder than
my wham-a-bama
one-man band.

I know what you're thinking: This is a poem for babies, and there is no way you are going to act like a fool, stomping around the classroom, patting your tummy, and playing imaginary cymbals.

Well, if you ever want to be funny or angry or sad in performance, you have to get over feeling silly moving around onstage.

Get up and get over it.

Here's another moving experience.

Have your class stand in a circle and play Pass the Movement. One jammer takes the lead and starts, let's say, by tapping his head. Everyone imitates his action. Then he passes the lead to the next jammer, and she chooses another movement, maybe rubbing her eyes or making windmill arms. Again, everyone copies her action. Proceed around the circle until everyone has had a chance to lead.

As you become more experienced with this game, you may choose more complex movements. For instance, say a jammer pretends to dig in the dirt to plant a flower, and everyone imitates that action. Now, talk about what this movement looks like.

Does it look as if people are "sewing" the soil?

Does it look as if people are making a flower castle in the dirt?

Comparing movements in this way will help not only your performance but your writing as well.

"Full Blast" is a poem that's just right for a chorus of jammers. Not a seat symphony but an on-your-feet symphony.

Can you think of some achy-breaky movements to put with this poem?

FULL BLAST

First day of vacation,
I busted a tooth.
First day at camp,
I got stitches.
First day at Grandma's,
I caught poison ivy,
which gave me the
all-over itches.

I went to the beach,
which sandblasted my eyes.
I stepped on a bee
and then broke out in hives.

All through the spring,
I was holding my breath
and counting the days.
Now,
I'm holding my breath
for these stupid X-rays.

Summer is three months of Saturdays!

It arrives too slow
and melts too fast.
At the starting gun,
I hit it full blast.
Now I hope it hangs on
'til I'm outta this cast.

In performance, always make your movements match the words of the poem.
No swaying, hair twisting, or rubbing your legs together like a cricket.
Unless the poem is about crickets.
Of course.

Voice Your Attitude

Did you ever notice how no two people look at things exactly the same? For instance, one person might see a flagpole and think it looks lonely. Someone else looking at the same flagpole might think it looks proud.

Any poem that is written for two voices has two different points of view—two different attitudes.

"Copycat" is a poem for two voices with attitude. Or it's a poem with attitude that you can perform with another person. (Depends on your attitude, I guess.)

So let's see how well you can perform with attitude. Partner up with another jammer, and repeat the first two lines of this poem back and forth. See how many different attitudes you can attach to those three little words.

COPYCAT

I'm serious.	*I'm serious.*
Don't copy me.	*Don't copy me.*
I mean it, now.	*I mean it, now.*
You let me be.	*You let me be.*
I'm outta here.	*I'm outta here.*
Don't follow me.	*Don't follow me.*
I'm warning you.	*I'm warning you.*
Stop.	*Stop.*
Stop.	*Stop.*
STOP.	*Stop that.*
Stop that.	*No fair.*
No fair.	*You better quit!*
You started it!	

Geez!

Now, divide the class into two teams—Team Red and Team Blue. Have each team of jammers take one half of "Copycat." Team Red will perform the words in the red box, Team Blue will take the words in the blue box. Everyone join together on the last word, *geez.*

Show some attitude in your performance. You can put your hands on your hips, point fingers, stick out your tongues. (How many times do you get an invitation to do *that* in school?) Take advantage of the opportunity here.

The next poem was born as a poem for a single voice, but I think it could evolve into a poem for two voices—with attitude. What do you think?

Partner up with another jammer and split the poem "A Choice" between the two of you. Have the rest of the class do the same.

Did everyone split the poem in the same way? No? Is that OK? Yes!

A CHOICE

You can scold,
or we can converse.
We can talk,
or we can curse.
Form a team,
or fight to be first . . .
but not both.

I can ask,
or I can demand.
Shake my fist,
or shake your hand.
We can walk together,
or take a stand . . .
but not both.

A state of mind,
a tone of voice.
Confrontation—cooperation,
a personal choice.
One or the other . . .
but not both.

When you want to convince someone to see things your way, it's always best to look them in the eye. Remember, the eyes of your audience will follow your eyes. You don't want them looking at the ceiling or (worse) at your feet. That's not a poetry jam, that's toe jam.

Yuck.

You Are Entitled to Your Point of View

Do you want to go through life as someone else's caboose? Of course not.

Do you want to follow your own track in life? Of course you do.

And who is in charge of expressing your point of view?

YOU!

When you express a point of view in performance, you want to convince the audience that you really mean it. No doubt. You want your view to ring true.

See if this exercise helps.

Complete this sentence with the name of your favorite writer:

I'm going to be as great as _____.

Now, choose another jammer to act as if he is arguing with you. The mock argument will go something like this:

> "I'm going to be as great as Langston Hughes."
> "I don't think so."
> "I'm going to be as great as Langston Hughes."
> "No way."
> "I'm going to be as . . ."

Your partner can vary her arguments, but keep repeating the same words. Feel your point of view gathering power inside of you and in your voice?

OK, now switch places and argue your partner into a more powerful performance.

Remember, a powerful voice is not necessarily a loud voice. It's just strong.

Now, try turning the poem "Steamed" into a poem for two voices. Divide the poem for performance with another jammer.

Be as powerful as a train engine when you state your point of view. Even if one of you adds some *clackety-clack, whoo-whoo* sound effects to this poem, stay strong.

STEAMED

I got it.
You've given me your view,
but my view is different.
No way
am I just your "me, too."

I don't like where we're going.
I'm not your caboose.
Uncouple yourself from my engine.
LET LOOSE!
Click-clack.
Look forward.
Click-clack.
Look back.
I'm not on your track, and
my whistle is fixin' to scream.
I'm warning you, Jack.
Peer pressure just makes me get
steamed.

When I write a poem, I go back in my mind to the experience that inspired the poem and feel the moment. Happy, sad, or disgusted, I have to feel it. Later, when I perform the poem, I go back to the same emotional place I was when I wrote it. Let yourself "feel the moment," and your words will ring true.

Don't just stand there: Stage your poem. Move with it. Cluster around it. Come together with a team of jammers, and then explode into different corners of the room.

Picture the stage as a giant tic-tac-toe grid. The power place on the stage is the middle square. But even more powerful than standing in one place is moving around. Poetry in motion is always more interesting. Poetry standing as still as a post is about as interesting as . . . well . . . a post.

Practice staging "Big Yellow Pain." Do you need chairs lined up like a school bus in the front of the room? Maybe. But everyone performs at the front of the room. How about staging your bus in the center of the room? Or better yet, put a line of jammers together, hands to shoulders, and move your bus around the room while performing the poem.

Lots of voices pop up in this poem. Divide them among your teammates. Who's in charge of sound effects on this one?

BIG YELLOW PAIN

THUMP, BUMP, BUMP
BOOM
This
BUMP, THUMP, THUMP
hurts.
SLAM
A backslap to start,
BAM
it stops me face first.
BUMP
The front's not that great,
WHAM
but the back is the worst!
JERKS
JUMP
Me bumping round corners.
SLIDES
SLIP
OOPS

Me side-to-side.
POP
PLOP
I'm just the pop balls
JOLT
DROP
on this pull-toy ride.
BOOM
BASH
It drops without warning,
WHAM!
springs me from the seat.
AIRBORNE!
AIRBORNE!
Tumble-turving my head
OOPS
HEADS UP
with my slam-dancing feet.
WHOA
CRASH
It scrambles my breakfast,
OOPS
YISH
and shock waves my spine
OUCH
SMASH
from my seat to my brain.
Scoo, scoo, school bus!
BAM!
CRASH.
You're a big yellow pain.

Poetry performance is a lot like sports. It's important to practice, and it's important to keep your body relaxed, especially your knees. Locking your knees will send quivers up and down your whole body.
Think of basketball players.
Think of runners at the starting line.
Think of swimmers taking their marks.
Stay loose.

Two's Good Company, but a Crowd Is Loud

Next, let me show you two poems that can be performed in groups of five or six jammers.

For the poem "Misery," you can split the lines up among some of the jammers, while other jammers can serve as the moaning, groaning chorus. Choose one jammer to be the coach of this piece. The coach's main job is to regulate volume so that the words rise above the chorus.

It's OK to moan throughout the piece, maybe with the volume rising and falling at certain points. Or you might want to punctuate certain lines with a moan. You get to choose—this is a community effort. But listen to what your coach tells you about the volume as you practice.

MISERY

If misery loves company,
then I could use a crowd—
a stadium of miserables
crying with me . . . loud!

Ten thousand people blubbering,
their twenty thousand eyes
swelled in tearful sympathy,
a woeful, wailing symphony,
audible a mile.
Then . . . maybe . . .
I would smile.

Now you're getting the idea of how to perform as a group.

Here is another poem that needs background noise—only this time the noise doesn't come from a chorus of miserables. It comes from constant

Dry your eyes and look at this: If you add movements to your performance, it will help you remember the words. When something pops up in front of your bike, you automatically jam on the brakes without thinking, right? That's muscle memory. If you build some muscle memories into your performance, it will help your word memory.
Meanwhile, use a tissue.
Really.

talking by one conversation hog. (Know the type? No names, please.)

To stage this piece, divide the lines up among some of the jammers. Choose one jammer to be the coach of this piece and one jammer to play Bruiser.

What is Bruiser so busy talking about? That's up to Bruiser. Improvise!

BRUISER DOESN'T LISTEN

Bruiser doesn't listen.
Just talks and talks.
Always.
Kind of makes you wonder
where he learned the
stuff he says.

His brain can't hear what's new
with his mouth on overdrive.
He doesn't stop to breathe.
It's a wonder he's alive.

He's the conversation hog
who always interrupts.
NEVER
ask for his advice.
He only knows what he makes up.

You could fill encyclopedias
with what he never hears.
He thinks I'm his best friend.
I haven't talked to him in years.

Don't start walking offstage as you recite the last line—especially in a poem such as this one, which ends with a punch line.
Stay put.
Deliver the last line.
Stay put.
Stay put.
Wait two counts before you move to exit. This is attention-seeking behavior at its best.

Going Solo

This is your chance to star in your own poetry production. You have been part of the chorus. You have played backup for other jammers. You have used your voice in different ways, practiced movement and staging.

It's time. Don't say you're not ready. It's time. Time for what? Time for you to perform on your own. That's what.

Here is a poem for practicing your dramatic solo jammin' presentation skills. Rehearse until you have it at least almost memorized. Give it some attitude. Give it your best.

APPEARANCES TO THE CONTRARY

I gripped my fists
and ran in place,
stuck out my tongue
and squinched my face.
Made boo-boo lip
and slammed the door,
crossed my arms
and stomped the floor.
You tried to talk,
I ran and hid.

Why do you
treat me
like a kid?

Do you remember the last time someone treated you like a little kid? Remember how that made you feel? Did the feeling bubble inside of you, or did it burn? Did it annoy you like a scratchy sweater? Let that memory become part of your performance. Feel the moment.

Here is another poem to move from the page to the stage. "Testing New Waters" has a stream in it—a stream with banks and swirling water passing by.

Imagine that stream. And then imagine you, standing on the edge.

Now, imagine you are trying to decide whether to test some new waters— maybe try out for a play, for instance. Or sing a solo or learn to tap dance. This is risky business!

Would you be scared? Would you be excited?

How do you communicate your emotion in performance?

And how do you stage this poem if you don't have a stream with swirling water in your classroom?

And what if your teacher says it's not OK to paint one on the floor?

Hey, I don't have all the answers. Don't look at me.

Look inside yourself.

Put a toe in—and swim.

TESTING NEW WATERS

Safely standing
on the bank of what-I-know,
unfamiliar water passing
in a rush.
If I jumped in,
would I float?
Or sink,
final as a flush?
I could paddle like a dog
and still wind up downstream.
What if I couldn't touch the bottom?
What if no one heard me scream?

I'm shackled to this doubtful bank
with maybes swirling in my ears.
It's hard to judge the depth
of an unknown stream of fears.

Fresh water gurgles by,
leaving me to wring my hands and look.
I could stand on what-I-know for life,
or I
could
test
one
foot.

Can you build some muscle memories
into this performance?
Can you wring your hands? Paddle like a dog?
Sniff. Sniff.
Put your socks back on. *Whew!*

Here are a couple of other poems to practice for your solo debut. Notice how each one reflects a different emotion. So many moods. Do you think you have them in you? All those whiny, wishing and hoping, sad, glad, and angry moods? You know you do.

JUST IMAGINE

Loves me . . .
Loves me not . . .
Loves me . . .
Loves me not . . .

The petal-popping,
forehead-bopping,
heartbeat-stopping
question.
Leaves me
sometimes singing,
then eyeballs stinging,
both hands wringing
crazy.

Is it love?
How can I know?
Just imagine
if it were so.

I'd be calm,
since I would *know*,
Love,
not craziness,
would grow.

This is a good poem to
act as your own boom
box. Keep a careful
hand on your volume
control. Let's see . . .
can you memorize
this one?
Just imagine.

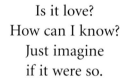

Just imagine
if it were so.
Just imagine
if it were so.

Just imagine if it were so!
Ah . . .

ANGRY

I'm angry.
Foot stomping,
door kicking,
wall hitting,
book throwing,
desk slapping,
drawer slamming,
pencil breaking,
teacher hating,
paper tearing,
teeth baring
mad.

After you are over your anger at yourself, try rewriting this poem. Change the title to "Excitement" or "Hopeful" or "Sad." You choose. Then rewrite the lines to match the emotion. The best part is, you can perform that, too.
How to do it?
It's up to you.

The worse part is,
can't you see?
There's no one else to blame
but me.

Here's a poem that is pretty short for performance. Can you improvise a little with this one, repeat some sounds, add an *ouch* or two to make the poem dance a little?

BAREFOOTING

Barefooting
over hot blacktop
electrocutes me on the street.
Short-circuiting
sense from my eyeballs
and signaling
GO!
to my feet.

Don't forget your entire tic-tac-toe grid on stage. How much of the stage can you use in this performance?

Developing a Split Personality

A poem for two voices can be performed by two jammers (as if you didn't know that already).

But did you know that a poem can also be performed by one jammer using two voices? Wacky? A little. But sometimes a little wacky is a good way to get your point across.

Wait—you don't think you have two voices in you? Try this.

Work with another jammer. Talk to that jammer as you would talk with a friend. Explain that you ate three candy bars for lunch today. Brag it up. You got away with something.

Now have your jammer partner appear as your mom. Pretend your mom just found your uneaten lunch in your bookbag after school. Explain to your mom that you ate three candy bars for lunch, using the same words as you did when you bragged to your friend.

Hear the difference in your two voices? Both voices are yours and the words are the same, but your tone and probably your body language have changed.

Changing your tone of voice will make you stand out in performance.

Not so sure? Well, think about someone droning on in the same monotone voice (a teacher, for instance). Doesn't that just make you want to sleep?

One of the major rules of performing is, "Never put the audience to sleep."

So practice changing your tone of voice on this poem. In "Old Pictures," the speaker is full of childish excitement at the start of the poem. Then the mood becomes more mature and thoughtful at the end. Try it out.

OLD PICTURES

See that hole in my smile
and the pat on my head?
I was so old
I could make my own bed.

I could pull on my boots,
zipper my clothes,
pick up my toys,
and tie my own bows.

I am much older
since I lost that tooth,
but you want to know
the honest-to-truth?

Grown up gets scary,
and that is a fact.
If I had a brain,
I'd have
put that tooth back.

Use movement also to show a change in this poem.
How would a proud little kid stand? How does that
stance change at the end of the poem?

Here is another poem that changes mood.

When I perform this poem, I begin in an excited "beach" voice, even though it is a serious poem about a sad time. Notice how the poem changes rhythm at the lines "Why does everything / have to go?" It kind of drops you flat.

Following these lines, I drop my voice in tone (making it deeper). And at that same point I also drop my body and sit on my heels. So the words, my voice, and my movements all come together to communicate that this experience has "dropped me low."

What movement and voice changes can you come up with to help communicate the meaning of the poem to your audience?

I HATE GOOD-BYE

I said good-bye
to the beach this year
with a pocket of shells
and a little tear.

When my friend moved away,
I smiled good-bye,
then I went to my room
for a private cry.

I hate good-bye.

It swells you up,
then leaves you low.
Why does everything
have to go?

When Molly went,
I curled on the floor,
like her,
in a heap.
And I smelled the place
where she used to sleep.
And I swore on the day
that old dog died
that I had said
my last good-bye.

Two Characters in One

Now that you have practiced changing your voice, can you change into an entirely different person—and change back again—all in the same poem?

In "May I Be Excused?"(on the next page), two different characters speak in the same poem—an ornery kid who is innocently telling stories at the dinner table, not really trying to be disgusting (OK, maybe trying a little), and a totally grossed-out grown-up lady.

Can you sound like an ornery kid? No problem, right?

Now, can you sound like a grown-up?

The trick to pulling this off is to not break character. That means, deliver the grown-up's lines in one voice and all the kid's lines in another voice—right up until the grown-up says the last two words, "How nice."

Does the kid hop around in excitement? Travel around the room while speaking? How does the grown-up put her fork down at the end of the poem?

This is up to your individual interpretation. That's if you can interpret two different individuals.

You may want to try this with a jammer partner first, and then try it on your own.

MAY I BE EXCUSED?

At dinner she said,
"Nice cat, is he yours?"

"Yeah, he is," I said.
"He hardly gets fur balls at all.
When he does?
He goes right outside to spit.
And he eats all his food
'fore the maggots get it,
most times."

I said, "Pass the rice.

"Once a dead squirrel
was behind the garage—
no one's fault, natural causes.
It was twelve times its size
'cause it swelled from the heat?
Kids came and saw it,
(ten cents a peek),
but the maggots got it
after a week or so, really sick."

I said, "Pass the meat.

"One summer
the trash cans got maggots
so bad I thought I would vomit.
So I called my dad,
who cleaned them himself
with a poison
he keeps on the shelf.
He said, if I touched it
my fingers would melt."

I said, "Pass the milk.

"I once touched a bird and got lice."

She put down her fork
and just said,
"How nice."

GET READY TO WHAM

A Word (or Two) About Contests

As long as people have walked on two legs, there have been contests to see who could walk the farthest, the fastest, or the straightest. People want to know how they stack up against others, whether they are playing the trombone in a band competition or running a mile. How else can you explain spelling bees?

Backyard gardeners, basketball players, loggers, fire fighters, hog callers, bird watchers, clowns, and hairdressers all have competitions. You can probably name dozens more.

Artists are no different. They compete in piano competitions, juried art shows, and film festivals and for book awards and theater prizes.

Performance poets and storytellers, sometimes called spoken-word artists, have their own forms of competition. This is a tradition that goes back not just years but centuries. In fact, winning poets who performed their work received laurel crowns at the Olympics in ancient Greece.

Can't you see how that began? One person told a story. And the next person said, "You think *that's* something? Well, listen to this!" And whoever received the most laughs or the most applause was declared the winner.

Poetry competition isn't just an item for the history books, though. Today, an annual poetry contest called Eisteddfod is held in Wales. A winner is crowned, and the event attracts thousands of folks. Theater games also are held in Australia for kids and grown-ups. I once competed in a poetry competition in Sweden, where poets performed in a boxing ring inside a huge field house.

So poetry contests occur today all over the world. People call them by different names: Poetry Slams, Poetry Jams, and there's at least one Poetry Circus. Each competition has its own traditions and rules, whether the contestants are rappers, cowboy poets, or writers of haiku. Some contests use points, some use applause. Some participants compete simply for the pleasure of seeing the biggest smiles on the faces of the audience.

One thing about competition: It can either inspire us to do better or discourage us from ever trying it again. A lot depends on how the competition is run.

In creating a performance-poetry competition for kids like you,

I wanted to make a game of the contest—a game that would inspire you not only to perform at your best but to write your own poetry.

And that's how WHAM was born.

Who Can Play?

Who can WHAM? You can. Your class can. The kids on your block or at your library can. You can WHAM solo. You can WHAM as a team, which rhymes with *scream*. . . . oh, don't get me started.

How Many Poets Make a Team?

Two, three, four, or half the class. The only rule is that in order to compete, you need at least two teams. I happen to think that team WHAMs are the most fun and the least likely to make your friends want to hide under their desks and never come out again.

The WHAM can be short—each team presenting one poem for multiple voices. In fact, this is a great place to start. Or the WHAM can be any combination of solo and group performances. For instance, a five-member team could have six trips to the stage: one for each individual team member and one for a group performance. As you become experienced WHAM jammers, you can think up new combinations.

How Do You Keep Score?

WHAM scoring is based on the scoring used for music competitions. This means that any performance can receive a score of 1, 2, or 3.
1: The jammer individual was first-rate, top drawer, doing his or her best.
2: The jammer individual was really, really good, but maybe he or she could improve by memorizing or performing a little more smoothly.
3: The jammer individual was good, but more practice would definitely help.

Then the individual scores are added up to make a team score. The lowest score wins (just like the way golf is scored).

You can also judge the entire team as one whole group with a score of 1, 2, or 3.

Who Can Judge?

Anyone who is not part of the WHAM competition can judge. It's a bad idea to have only one judge. That's too much pressure on one person. It's best to have three or five judges. If you choose five, you can throw out the top score and the bottom score, just as they do in the Olympics. To choose judges, you can pull names out of a hat. Or pick one or two "celebrity" judges (the student teacher down the hall, another class, the principal). But it is always a good idea to have some kids as judges if other kids are competing. Who else can really tell if a team is slacking off or giving its best effort?

Judges can either write their scores down and pass them to the scorekeeper in private, or they can hold up one, two, or three fingers.

What Are the Rules of the Game?

Get all jammers together as a community to agree on WHAM rules. (They could be different for each WHAM and for each group.) Write them down beforehand. (Can you imagine a baseball game without the three-strikes-and-you're-out law?) The rules should remain the same throughout the WHAM.

Every rule should also have a penalty attached to it if the rule is violated (for instance, a point added for going over a time limit.)

Go over the rules—*out loud*—before each event, so jammers aren't surprised if they are penalized for a violation.

Your jammin' community may even want to have specific rules for specific contests. For example, you might want your next WHAM competition to consist of only poems with refrains, or only haiku, or only poems about reptiles, or only poems by dead poets, or only poems written by the performers.

Here are some sample rules you might want to use:

Time limits. Most poetry contests have time limits. This prevents one poet from droning on for 17.5 minutes, which not only can be a real snore for the audience but, in a school situation, might delay the buses or *(gasp)* lunch. For starters, I would suggest a two- or three-minute time limit.

Penalty: How about adding a half point to the score for going over the time limit?

School rules. No poetry competition should break school rules. This includes using lazy language like foul words (you know which ones I'm talking about) or showing disrespect for or hurting another jammer or school property.

Penalty: Penalties are in place for violating school rules. I suggest you follow those. If you do not penalize the offending jammer for breaking a school rule, you can expect that the entire class will lose their poetic privileges for WHAM competition. What fun is that?

Team jam versus solo jam. Both can be fun, but be sure you decide in advance which one will be performed. Basically, there are poems for multiple voices and poems for solo voices. You might want to enact a rule that if a team member shouts out words to a poem during another team member's solo performance, then that becomes a poem for multiple voices.

Penalty: I'd suggest a one- or two-point addition for breaking this rule. It's a real no-no.

Background music, drums, kazoos, or costumes. This can be fun—or really confusing. I tend to favor just sticking to the words, but combining words and music is an old tradition. Your community can make up its own mind.

Penalty: Playing a trumpet in a poetry WHAM in which musical instruments are outlawed is pretty much over the top. That might qualify for disqualification.

Singing. This is OK, as long as you are singing the words to the poem, not "Over the Rainbow." Remember, it's a poetry WHAM, not a top-ten countdown. Sometimes it's fun to sing or hum a little of a song to set up a poem. For instance, you might hum a few bars of "Take Me Out to the Ball Game" to set up a poem about baseball. But singing the entire song instead of reciting a poem would be a WHAM violation.

Penalty: Maybe a one-point addition, but you might leave this up to the judges.

Applause. Always applaud the WHAM jammer.

Who Is in Charge? You are—and every other jammer and audience member. This is a community event without one boss. If you are enforcing a time limit, it is best to choose one person to watch the clock. Another jammer can serve as scorekeeper. One jammer may serve as emcee to introduce the competitors during the WHAM. Another jammer can hold up an applause sign after every poem.

What If There Is a Tie? This is your WHAM, remember? Maybe ties are OK. Maybe you want to create a sudden-death tiebreaker. Maybe everybody *deserved* a score of 1 that day, and your class should order pizza and have a celebration.

Now you are ready to WHAM. You are ready to jam. You are ready to have some fun.

Practice team and solo performances with the poems included in this book. But don't stop there. Choose other poems by your favorite poets. Check out the library. Check Internet sites for poems by other kids. Check your sock drawer for poems you wrote last year. Write new poems. Plan a WHAM competition. And let the words explode all over the class.

Following are some practice poems that you can combine for group jammin'. Other poems can be recited as written for solo performances or with two or more voices. Use them at will. Practice, practice, practice. But remember, these are just stepping stones to the ultimate show of words—you WHAMMIN' and JAMMIN' with your own poetry.

Creating Poems for Multiple Voices

Sometimes a poet makes it easy on the performer and writes a poem for two voices. Sometimes two poets get together and combine separate poems into one for two voices.

Say two jammer poets have written poems on a similar subject. Say the subject is "my favorite sport." Say they want to combine the two poems into one performance.

Can they perform the poems one right after the other? Can they trade lines back and forth? Can they edit the poems to make them fit together better? Can they add new lines? Can they repeat lines as refrains? Can they speak solo? Can they speak in unison?

Yes to all the above!

Two separate poems are shown on page 43. On page 44, I combined them into one performance piece.

Is this the *only* way they might be put together?

No.

You may read the poems and see them coming together differently. Once you combine two different poems into a performance piece, add a new title. But save the original poems. They still have a life of their own.

GYMNAST

Stick the landing,
        for the team, all alone,
no dancing around
        in my end zone.
Concentration—
        grip the bars,
pull up and over,
        reach for the stars.
The strength to be delicate,
        floor routines,
the mat, myself,
        the balance beams.
Scoring points,
        Olympic dreams.

BASEBALL PLAYER

Grip bat.
Cap down.
Adjust stance.
Tap the ground.
Knees bent.
Muscles tense.
Eye on the ball.
Swing. *Smack!*
Round the bases.
Touch them all.

Scoring a run
on my own.
I'm major league.
Sliding home.

Two separate opinions, two separate poems. Look at what is different between them. Look at what is the same. Turn the page, and look at how they can come together like folded fingers.

TITLE NEEDED

Stick the landing,

           Sliding home.

for the team,

           on my own.

There's no dancing around

           Cap down.

           Adjust stance.

in my end zone.

           Knees bent.

           Tap the ground.

Concentration—

           Eye on the ball.

grip the bars,

           Grip the bat.

pull up and over,

           Swing. *Smack!*

      for the stars.

The strength to be delicate,

           Muscles tense.

floor routines,
the mat, myself,

           Round the bases.

           Touch them all.

the balance beam.

           A winning team.

Scoring points,

           Major league.

Olympic dreams.
Stick the landing.

           Sliding home.

Remember, there is no right way or wrong way to combine poems. This is not a proficiency test.

But I'm confident you *will* become proficient at creating performance pieces by combining poems. Practice on these, and then experiment with your own poetry.

Don't have anything in your notebook that you think would work?

Write something!

Merging Unlike Poems

Poems are as unique as snowflakes—or, you might say, as unique as the poets who wrote them. Even if poets have different opinions, you might still find a way to combine their poems. It's a way of conducting a debate.

To combine them, look for what the poems have in common, and look at the differences. Reorder, recycle, repeat, and revise.

Since all poems are not created equal when it comes to length, feel free to punch up a shorter poem with extra lines in order to give the performance piece balance. You could trade some lines back and forth, too. See how two poems, which look as if they are mismatched in size and opinions, can "cooperate" with each other.

COOPERATION

Cooperation is hard,
and it's work
to make caring last.
Sometimes,
forgiveness is tough to chew,
and understanding melts too fast.

I could always order it my way,
that's easy.
I could protect
me first and only.
I could never compromise.
But stubborn gets,
well,
lonely.

WHAT'S FAIR?

It's not fair.
I have to share
my games, my bike, my sweater.
It's not right
that parents fight.
Isn't there a better
way to stay
than in this family way?

It's tempting just to hate
the word
cooperate
when you're arguing who's boss.
It's too bad
the times we had
to listen through tight jaws.

Some of my maddest times
I think,
alone's the way to live.
And other times I'm glad
I have
a family to forgive.

WHO'S BOSS?
(You have a better title? Use that!)

It's not fair.
I have to share—

I have to share my games,
my bike, my sweater.

Cooperation is hard.

It's not right
that parents fight.

That's hard.

That's hard.

Isn't there a better
way to stay
than in this family way?

Cooperation is hard,
and it's work
to make caring last.

It's tempting just to hate
that word.

That word . . . *cooperate?*

when you're arguing who's boss.
Some of my maddest times
I think,
alone's the way to live.

Sometimes,
forgiveness is tough to chew,

And other times I'm glad
I have
a family to forgive

Sometimes understanding
melts too fast.

I could always order it my way,

           that's easy.

I could protect
me first

           Me first.

ME first.

           ME first
           and only.

I could never compromise.

           Cooperation is hard.
Yeah, but stubborn gets,   well,
lonely.   lonely. *(together)*

PERFORM ON

Here are a few more poems with tiger teeth and tippy-toe feet to keep you busy until you start performing your own poems.

A *GOOD* FAIRY

When I'm in trouble
I don't need
gossamer wings,
sugary sweet,
starry wands,
or tippy-toe feet.

I need a good fairy,
belching fire
through tiger teeth,
a charging bull,
eyes glowing.
King Kong,
sumo stomping
with grizzly bear claws,
and wings
like a Boeing.

GOOD SHOW

The fact I see no need to hurry
    while
      wandering
         through
     daydreams
puts my mother in a fury.

She calls and begs and screams.

Her power surge is quite impressive.
We both know
that I can hear it.
Whew, is she expressive.
I just
stand
and
stare
in
awe.

No joke.
You gotta admire
her spirit.

BETTER THAN?

The snob
hides behind
a designer exterior,
putting down others
and acting superior.

He's
the smoothest,
the richest,
most likely to win.
Which he'll tell you
before
you can even ask him.

He's
constantly buffing
his wax of perfection.
He shines
from a distance
but
not
(look close),
not not,
definitely
not
on
closer
inspection.

ME, TOO

Are you normally weird
and strangely the same?
Are you lost and found
with a nervy brain?
Is your rewind fast-forward?
Are you up front from the back?
Are you stuck?
And unglued?
Just a little bit cracked?
Do you never want your beginnings to end?

WAIT!
One more thing—

Will you be my friend?

The original version of "Better Than?" reads:
He shines
from a distance
but
not
on
closer
inspection.
See how I punched up the performance
version to leave more room for physical and
comical interpretation? This is like improvising
on a trumpet or a guitar in a musical piece.
It's fun to play the words in different ways.

TO BE SURE

That dragon of mine!
He pester-pester-pesters.
He's self-conscious
and unsure.
He drags at my feet,
is moody and shy,
and always suspects the worst.

He likes to
swirl my head
around
around.
He's a humorless beast
who confuses my brain
and breaks me down.

On the dragon's day off,
my hair stays put.
I can't be tripped
by word or look.
The whole world laughs,
but not at me.
I stand my ground
like a supple tree.

BLUEPRINTS?

Will my ears grow long as Grandpa's?
What makes us look like kin?
Tell me where'd I get long eyelashes
and where'd I get my chin?

Where'd I get my ice-cream sweet tooth
and this nose that wiggles when I talk?
Where'd I get my dizzy daydreams
and my foot-rolling, side-step walk?

Did I inherit my sense of humor
and these crooked, ugly toes?
What if I balloon like Uncle Harry
and have to shave my nose?

How long after I start growing
until I start to shrink?
Am I going to lose my teeth
someday?
My hair?
My mind?
Do you think
I'll be tall or short or thin
or bursting at the seams?
Am I naturally this crazy?
Is it something in my genes?

I'm more than
who I am,
I'm also
who I'm from.
It's a scary speculation—
Who will I become?

"Mr. Who" is a puzzle poem. It can be fun to perform, especially if you fool the audience by saying the first line in a low and spooky voice.

Keep them guessing for as long as possible about the true identity of Mr. Who.

MR. WHO

We have a ghost in our house,
we call him Mr. Who.
Who does all the things
a kid would never do.

Like put trays in the freezer
with no water or no ice.
Any kid would know
that wasn't very nice.

Who uses toilet paper
but doesn't change the roll,
eats cereal by the T.V.
and then steps in the bowl.

Who leaves his trucks and cars
spread out on the floor.
When Daddy walks in barefoot,
Who hides behind the door.

Who won't take time to flush,
forgets to feed the cat,
always hides my shoes,
and never puts milk back.

Who doesn't make the bed,
and when it's time for chores?
Who thinks it's kind of cute
to drag me out-of-doors.

And so I get in trouble.
What's a kid to do?
"Who did this?" they ask.
I shrug.
"Well, you know Who!"

A QUESTION OF PHYSICS

Oops!
Out of hand,
such wasted potential.
Off the wall,
experimental.
Bouncy, bright,
and so well rounded,
could be bubbly but
not if grounded.
How far can a gumball roll?

Holy molecules!
Look at it go—
force times distance,
momentum released
across six rows,
beneath twelve seats.
My pulse compounds,
I map the direction—
velocity minus the odds of detection,
factoring for mounting friction,
multiplied by heat
and teacher tension.
Matter out of control
could spell detention!
How far can a gumball roll?

BLOWN AWAY

There was never a rep like Tony's.
His was the coldest in the school.
In the library?
Check it out.
His picture's under *cool.*
He was exclusive,
an original,
we copied him
from his hair down to his stroll.
That was,
till Tony joined the Panthers
and the gang ate Tony whole.

Now, he wears their look,
their jacket,
their shoes,
their hat,
and their tatoos.
He must have Dumpster-tossed his brain.
He even wears their attitudes.

The Panthers
tell him where to go,
how to talk, and
what to say.
Tony better get a grip
before he's blown away.

ALONE

Alone
doesn't have to be sad
like a lost-in-the-city dog.

Alone
doesn't have to be scary
like a vampire swirled in fog.

Alone
can be slices of quiet,
salami in between
a month of pushy hallways
and nights too tired to dream.

Alone
doesn't have to be
a scrimmage game with grief.
Alone
doesn't have to argue,
make excuses, or compete.
Like having nothing due,
sometimes.
Alone
is a relief.

52

THE STORM THAT WAS

Me?
I rolled in like a storm,
darkening the room,
ominously rumbling,
then erupting with a BOOM!

I HATE PEOPLE.
I HATE SCHOOL.
I HATE WHAT'S HOT.
I HATE WHAT'S COOL.
I CAN'T STAND RIDING BUSES.
ALL MY FRIENDS ARE MEAN.
THE WORLD IS GUACAMOLE
                AND
I HATE THE COLOR GREEN.

And you?
You didn't run for cover
or have that much to say.
You listened to my cloudburst.

And the storm?
It blew away.

THE FINAL ACT

Poets look for truth. They are lifelong kids in the sense that they are never afraid to say the Emperor has no clothes—even if the poet is the Emperor.

Does that mean I am suggesting you strip and go naked when performing poetry?

NO! I don't think so.

Definitely not.

I don't even want to see your underwear. Whether you are performing your own poems or someone else's, you want to keep the focus on the words.

A good performer, like a good poet, tries to strip away some of the pretense, the fake smiles that cover hurt, the little lies we tell to cover up.

You want to show what's really true.

This book has no real conclusion, because the fun never stops when you are performing poetry.

Take your poetry out of the classroom,
    to the class next door,
        to the gym.

WHAM!

Show the world that poetry was never meant to simply lie quietly on the page, any more than kids were meant to sit quietly in their seats to read it.

Have fun with the words.

Make them your own.

See you onstage!

A NOTE TO POETRY JAM COORDINATORS

Just as writing is a process, so is performance. If you are careful to lay out these few beginner steps for your jammers, they will soon dance all over the stage, up the walls, and across the ceiling.

A poetry jam is a lesson in language, communication, and presentation skills. Everybody wants to be heard, and poetry performance gives participants a chance to express themselves as individuals. Poetry performance also inspires poets to put words on paper and encourages them to refine their writing.

But the benefits don't stop there. It is a lesson in group-management skills. It is a lesson in cooperation and mutual respect. If the jammers are truly able to assume responsibility for managing the poetry action, then it is a working lesson in democracy.

Have fun, and then stand back and let the poetry jam happen.